First published in Great Britain in 2023 by Orion Fiction,
an imprint of The Orion Publishing Group Ltd.,
Carmelite House, 50 Victoria Embankment
London EC4Y 0DZ

An Hachette UK Company

1 3 5 7 9 10 8 6 4 2

A CIP catalogue record for this book is available from the British Library.

ISBN (Paperback) 978 1 4091 9241 1
ISBN (eBook) 978 1 4091 9242 8

Typeset by Input Data Services Ltd, Somerset

Printed and bound in Great Britain by Clays Ltd, Elcograf S.p.A.

MIX
Paper from responsible sources
FSC® C104740

www.orionbooks.co.uk

BLACK FELL

Stone and Oliver Series

Book 4

MARI HANNAH

ORION